GIRLS SURVIVE

Girls Survive is published by Stone Arch Books
A Capstone Imprint
1710 Roe Crest Drive
North Mankato, Minnesota 56003
www.capstonepub.com

Text and illustrations © 2020 Stone Arch Books

Library of Congress Cataloging-in-Publication Data
Names: Berne, Emma Carlson, author. | Forsyth, Matt, illustrator. | Trunfio, Alessia, 1990–
artist.
Title: Ruth and the Night of Broken Glass : a World War II survival story / by Emma
Carlson Berne ; illustrated by Matt Forsyth ; cover art by Alessia Trunfio
Other titles: Girls survive.
Description: North Mankato, Minnesota : Stone Arch Books, [2019] | Series: Girls survive |
Summary: In November 1938, young Ruth Block is a Jewish girl in Frankfurt, Germany,
trying to cope with the ever-tightening noose of Nazi oppression. Her father's stationery
store has been shut down, and her school closed. Then one night her family's apartment
is broken into, and her father is dragged out, arrested, and taken to a concentration
camp. It becomes clear that if Ruth and her best friend, Miriam, are going to survive,
they must somehow get out of Germany, even if it means leaving their parents behind.
Identifiers: LCCN 2019008757| ISBN 9781496583871 (hardcover) | ISBN 9781496584496
(pbk.) | ISBN 9781496583925 (ebook pdf)
Subjects: LCSH: Kristallnacht, 1938—Juvenile fiction. | Kindertransports (Rescue
operations)—Juvenile fiction. | Jewish girls—Germany—Frankfurt am Main—Juvenile
fiction. | Survival—Juvenile fiction. | Frankfurt am Main (Germany)—History—20th
century—Juvenile fiction. | Germany—History—1933–1945Juvenile fiction. | CYAC:
Kristallnacht, 1938—Fiction. | Jews—Germany—Frankfurt am Main—Fiction. |
Survival—Fiction. | Frankfurt am Main (Germany)—History—20th century—Fiction. |
Germany—History—1933–1945—Fiction. | LCGFT: Historical fiction.
Classification: LCC PZ7.B7576 Ru 2019 | DDC 813.6 [Fic]—dc23
LC record available at https://lccn.loc.gov/2019008757

Designer: Charmaine Whitman

Cover art: Alessia Trunfio

Image credits: Newscom: Pictures From History, 107; Shutterstock: Max Lashcheuski
(background), 2 and throughout; Tom Uhlman, 112; XNR Productions, 105

The author is grateful to Dr. Alan E. Steinweis, Professor of
History and Miller Distinguished Professor of Holocaust Studies at
the University of Vermont, for answering many questions about
Kristallnacht and daily life in Frankfurt, Germany, 1938.

Printed in the United States   4944

RUTH
AND THE
NIGHT OF BROKEN GLASS
A World War II Survival Story

by Emma Carlson Berne

illustrated by Matt Forsyth

WITHDRAWN

STONE ARCH BOOKS
a capstone imprint

CHAPTER ONE

"Miriam!" I knocked on the carved wooden door at the back of my best friend's apartment.

The door swung open, and Miriam stood there, slightly out of breath and covered with flour. Behind her, I could see her mother in the kitchen, mixing something in a bowl. Her father, Rabbi Gluck, was sitting at the table, hunched over two huge Talmudic texts. His long, black beard almost brushed the surface. It was a familiar sight. Rabbi Gluck was the rabbi for our synagogue—really our whole neighborhood—so he was often studying religious books.

"Want to go with me to get butter?" I asked. "Mama's making the cake for my party tonight, and she just ran out."

"Are you excited to turn twelve, bubbeleh?" Mrs. Gluck asked as she kneaded the challah dough.

"Yes, Mrs. Gluck," I replied.

She smiled at me, then turned to Miriam. "Miriam, you might as well go," she said. "You're getting as much flour on yourself as into the dough."

Miriam grinned at me and grabbed her coat. Together we hurried back out the door. Out on the sidewalk, we brushed through the busy crowds that always lined the sidewalks of our Frankfurt neighborhood.

"So, who's coming to the party?" Miriam asked.

We wound our way around a man in a Nazi uniform making a speech. There were so many gray and brown uniforms on the streets now, not to mention swastika flags with the red background and the twisted black cross. Papa said they were all over Germany. I was used to them at this point, but they never failed to make me uneasy.

"Everyone in our class!" I said, pausing at a stack of newspapers outside the grocer.

I felt angry—and a little sick to my stomach—when I saw the front page. On the very top of the pile, a large cartoon showed an octopus with a twisted-up face grasping the globe with all eight of his tentacles. A Jewish star floated above the octopus's head, and black goo dripped from its arms.

"What does it mean?" I asked.

"Jews are strangling the world, I guess," Miriam said beside me.

We looked at each other, and I could tell Miriam felt as upset as I did. Lately the newspapers seemed to carry more and more anti-Jewish cartoons and articles. Papa had said it was Joseph Goebbels. Fürher Hitler had appointed him head of the Ministry of Public Enlightenment and Propaganda. Goebbels didn't like Jews. None of the Nazis did.

"It's not right, saying things like that," I said furiously. I flung the newspaper facedown so neither Miriam nor I could see the cartoon anymore.

"Those cartoons are everywhere lately. I hate seeing them," Miriam murmured.

I put my arm through hers and pulled her toward the grocer. "I know," I said. "But we're *not* disgusting octopuses or whatever that was. And it's not OK for them to say so. I don't care how important they are."

The bell over the grocer's door tinkled as Miriam and I entered the store. We'd shopped for food here since I was a baby. Frau Hermann was not Jewish, so her shop wasn't kosher, but Mama always sent us to buy dairy and vegetables there.

Frau Hermann was behind the counter, arms crossed over her ample middle, as always. When she saw us, her face tightened into a frown.

"Hello!" I greeted her as we approached the counter. "How is Helga?" Frau Herrmann's daughter, Helga, was just a couple of years younger than Miriam and me.

"There is no need to ask after Helga," Frau Hermann said shortly. Her voice was oddly strangled. She shot a glance over her shoulder toward the back room. "What do you want?" she snapped.

"Ah, b-butter," I stammered, stung and bewildered by her harsh tone. It was drastically different from her normal, friendly voice.

Frau Hermann opened the icebox and practically threw a block of paper-wrapped butter across the counter. "Take it and get out. Don't come back. You're not welcome here anymore."

I just stood there in front of the counter, my mouth open. "What? Why not?" I asked. Beside me, Miriam whimpered once, like a kicked dog.

Frau Hermann leaned on the counter, bringing her face closer to us. "Jews are not allowed to purchase in the shops anymore," she said. "The SA came to tell us this morning."

I shuddered at the mention of Hitler's storm troopers. They were like soldiers and policemen rolled into one.

"But we've been coming here my whole life!" I protested.

Frau Hermann pinched her lips and looked toward the door. "No Jews," she repeated.

"That's not fair. Why?" I repeated. The same anger I'd felt at the newspaper cartoon rose in me, and my voice rose along with it.

"There's bad trouble coming," she said. "Be careful. The SA are everywhere."

Before I could say anything else, the door was open again, and Frau Hermann was pushing us out into the street. Behind us, the door slammed with a furious tinkling of the bell.

Out on the sidewalk, Miriam and I stared at each other in shock.

"I can't believe this!" I said. "We're not allowed to buy food in her store? This can't be right!" I was squeezing the butter so hard my fingernails punched through the paper.

"Ruth, I'm scared," Miriam said. "The SA—"

"The SA are not gods!" I snapped. "What gives them the right to say where we cannot buy things?"

Miriam was quiet for a moment. Finally she said, "Let's just try to forget it. We have a party to dress for—or did you forget?"

I took a deep breath, trying to steady myself. "I remember." Miriam was right. I had a party to get ready for.

Together we hurried up the street toward home. We reached Miriam's apartment first.

"I'll see you in a bit," I said. With a final wave, I headed for my own apartment.

"Did you get the butter?" Mama called as I came up the stairs.

I paused in the hallway, still clutching the cool package. *Should I tell her what happened?* I wondered.

No, I decided. She would just get upset. Then I would get upset. And what I really wanted to do was forget Frau Hermann and focus on my party.

"Yes!" I called.

"Well, hurry and get ready," Mama said. She bustled out from the kitchen and took the butter from me.

I did as I was told, going to my room and putting on my nicest party dress, the one with the blue ribbons at the neck and hem.

When I came back out, Mama had set the cake, now beautifully frosted, in the middle of the table. It was surrounded by dishes of nuts, pickles, and a platter of little tuna sandwiches.

I filled the big crystal pitcher with lemonade and set out my favorite ruby-colored napkins. Everything looked perfect. Now all I needed was guests.

"Sit down!" Mama ordered me, after watching me rearrange the nut bowls for the third time. "They'll be here any—"

Her words were cut off by the *brriiingg!* of the doorbell.

"They're here!" I cried, rushing downstairs. I opened the door to find Miriam and Isaac, our friend from class.

"Happy birthday!" Isaac said. He handed me a big paper-wrapped lollipop. His hair was combed neatly over to one side, and he wore a light-gray wool jacket and knickers.

"Thank you. You're the first ones here," I told them, leading them up the stairs.

Mama talked with us while we waited for the rest of my classmates to arrive. I listened carefully for the doorbell, but the minutes ticked by, and still it didn't ring. Finally Mama went to the window and pulled back the lace curtain, peering down into the street.

"Where *is* everyone?" I felt close to tears. The party was supposed to have started an hour ago, and fifteen children weren't here.

"I . . . I'm not sure they're coming," Isaac said slowly. "I heard some kids talking about this at school yesterday."

"Talking about what?" I demanded.

"Gentile kids aren't allowed to associate with Jewish kids anymore," Isaac said. "Their parents are keeping them away. Herr Hitler has been speaking out against Aryans associating with Jews."

Miriam and I looked at each other. We were both thinking of what happened at Frau Hermann's shop.

"That's disgusting!" I cried. Angrily, I wiped away the tears that had spilled down my cheeks.

Mama put her arm around me from one side, and Miriam did the same from the other.

"Herr Hitler made his speech yesterday," Isaac said. "Everything's different now."

CHAPTER TWO

At school the next day, I couldn't stop thinking
about my party. I kept looking at all the Gentile
children in my classroom, wanting to say something,
but no one would meet my eyes. I remembered
what Mama had said last night, as I lay twisting
the blankets up in my bed.

"Things are bad right now for Jews, Ruth," she'd
told me. "But this madman Hitler can't last. Your
papa is sure of that. But we mustn't say anything
to anyone." She'd smoothed my hair away from
my forehead. "It's important *not to make trouble.*

Do you understand? Do not speak of this to your classmates."

"Why?" I'd demanded.

Mama's face had closed off. "Your papa thinks it's best. He has seen some arrests. Jews who have spoken out against this prejudice."

"Arrests?" I'd bolted up in bed.

"Sha-sha-sha." Mama had eased me back onto the pillow. "We will be safe if we are quiet. Now rest."

And so, all day at school, I stayed quiet. But my insides were a tangled mess of fear and anger.

Why is this happening to us? I thought. *We haven't done anything except live our lives the same as always. What gives people the right to treat us this way, like we're worms?*

I ground my teeth as Herr Muller droned on at the front of the room. But I stayed quiet.

After school, out in the bright sunshine with Miriam, I felt a little better. We walked briskly, swinging our books in their straps. Miriam carried her blue-and-silver prayer book separately in her arms. Her father had given it to her when she was six years old, and she almost never went anywhere without it.

As we turned on the main street, Miriam stopped and gasped. She grabbed my arm so hard it hurt.

"Ow!" I exclaimed. "What?"

Miriam pointed. All up and down the street, huge red-and-black letters were painted on storefront after storefront: *Jude.* Jew.

Only the Jewish stores had been painted, I realized. *Jude. Jude. Jude.* There were huge Stars of David too, the paint slopped on, running down like tears.

I saw the words and stars over and over again, slapped on windows and above doors. The kosher butcher, the hardware store, Chaim Blumenthal's law office, the bakery where we bought cookies for Shabbat. All closed. All locked tight.

Here and there, little knots of men and women stood talking quietly, glancing uneasily over their shoulders. Miriam and I looked at each other. Fear crawled in my stomach.

"Papa. Papa's usually at his shop right now," I whispered.

My father had a stationery store two blocks away. He was usually there doing the accounts in a ledger, staring at paper samples, or talking to customers.

Miriam grabbed my arm and we took off, almost running down the street. The policemen strolled up and down, glancing at the pedestrians.

We turned the block. My feet pounded the cobblestones. The breath was whistling in my tight chest. Another block—more stores, all closed, shut tight like death.

We rounded the corner. There, in the middle of the row, I saw Papa's shop. *JUDE* screamed at me from across the front. We crept closer and peered in. There was a gaping hole in the front window. A big rock was lying inside, on the floor—someone had thrown it through the window.

Miriam and I stood together trembling, holding hands, not speaking. A few pieces of stationery drifted toward us on the wind, pulled out of the broken window by the Frankfurt breeze.

Where is Papa? I thought.

"Papa!" I burst in the door of the apartment and threw myself into his arms as soon as I saw him at the table.

Papa set down his cup of tea and smoothed my hair as I buried my face in his shirt.

"The shop!" I cried. "It's ruined!" I pulled back and looked from him to Mama. "What happened? Who did this?"

Papa shook his head. "A few bad people encouraged by the SA."

"We have to do something!" I exclaimed angrily. "They can't just get away with this. We have to fight back."

"Ruth, *bubbeleh*, try not to be angry," Papa said. "Yes, this is bad. But surely, this is the worst. This was just a few prejudiced people—they are the ones causing all this trouble. But our friends, our neighbors—these people are not doing these terrible things."

I looked at Papa, and for the first time I noticed the white bandage stuck over his left eye. "Papa, did they hurt you?" I exclaimed.

Papa glanced over my head at Mama.

"How did they—what happened, Papa? How could they?"

I was interrupted by a hurried tapping at the back door. I opened it to find Miriam and her mother.

"Oh, Ruth, such trouble," Mrs. Gluck said as she pushed past me into the room. She was visibly shaken. "Gitla, Mendel, I'm so glad you're here. Mendel, your store!"

Papa shook his head. "Vandalism, that's all."

"It's the SA—they hate all Jews," I broke in.

Mrs. Gluck glanced at me. "It's not just the stores," she replied. "Miriam and I are going to the American consulate. We must see if we can get visas. We need to get out! Who knows what these Nazis will do next?"

Leave the country? I thought. I glanced at Miriam, my eyes wide.

She nodded. "Mama is determined," she whispered. "Papa says he can't leave the congregation and the synagogue, but she says we will try to go anyway."

"Rochel, surely that can't be necessary," Mama said, putting a hand on Mrs. Gluck's arm. "Please, let's stay calm. This is the worst, surely."

"We have to stay and fight back," I said. "We can't just run away."

Mrs. Gluck ignored me. "Gitla, the time for staying calm is past! It will be a pogrom, just like Odessa! We need to get out!"

I knew about the pogroms in the Russian Empire at the turn of the century. Older people in the synagogue often talked about them, and Rabbi Gluck had spoken about Odessa in his sermons. The Russian Jews had seen their villages burned and had been driven from their homes. Many of them had escaped to Britain and the United States.

Papa spoke up: "The Blochs will stay, Rochel. But we wish you good luck at the consulate."

"But, Mendel, what about the letter?" Mama asked quietly.

"What letter?" I asked.

Papa sighed and slowly withdrew a sheet of paper from his pocket. "It's a letter I received from a friend in France. He said he has a feeling . . ."

"Speak up, Mendel!" Mrs. Gluck interrupted. "What are you saying?"

Papa unfolded the letter and smoothed it, gazing down at the spidery writing. "He says to get out.

He says things will become very bad here. He has a bad feeling and wants to warn us. But I cannot believe the good people of Germany would allow anything worse to happen."

"We won't let them!" I clenched my fists on my knees. "We'll fight them! They can't do this, Papa."

"See!" Mrs. Gluck said. "You must come! Please!"

"No," Papa said firmly. "I need to open my shop again. When we are allowed, at least. I am too old to start again in a new country."

Mrs. Gluck gathered her bag and hat. "I've tried my best. Come, Miriam. We must go before it gets much later."

"Please, can't you come with us?" Miriam whispered to me, her eyes begging.

"Papa, can I go?" I burst out. "Just to keep Miriam company."

Mama and Papa exchanged a look, but he nodded. "Don't get into any trouble," he said. "And come straight back—don't go anywhere else."

Out on the sidewalk, I shivered against the damp November chill. I bent my head as Miriam, her mother, and I quickly walked the half-mile to the square where the American consulate stood. I could see the big brick building ahead. But there was something outside.

At first, I thought it was a new wall, made of something black. But it was moving. Then I realized what I was looking at—people, lined up outside of the consulate, packed so tightly together that no daylight was visible between them.

"Is it not open then? People are waiting at the door?" Mrs. Gluck asked as we approached.

But the door was open—propped open, in fact. People spilled out and down the street. The line outside continued around the block.

"All these people are trying to get out?" Miriam asked, voicing the question that was already in my head.

"I'll go see what's going on," I offered. "You go get in line."

I left Miriam and Mrs. Gluck at the back of the line and ducked and pushed my way to the doorway. I followed the snaking line of people up the stairs. Down a long hallway, then another hallway, then into a huge reception room where the line wound round and round.

Everyone was packed together, clutching papers. The room smelled of damp wool. Everywhere I looked, faces were drawn and frightened.

I stood near the door of the reception room, tracing the line back with my mind. So many people. So many worried faces. *Hundreds?* I thought. *A thousand?* I could smell the desperation in the room. What did they know that I didn't?

CHAPTER THREE

Frankfurt, Germany
Ruth's apartment
November 9, 1938

I clung to Mama the next morning when it was time to leave for school. I hadn't done that since I was six. But after yesterday I didn't want to go out on the street alone. Not after what had happened to Papa's store. Not after what I'd seen at the consulate.

"Now, stop. There is nothing to worry about," Mama said, pushing a warm onion roll into my hand. "Get along to school. Look, Miriam is already down on the sidewalk, waiting."

I peered out the window beside us and saw Miriam's bright-red beret on the street below and her arms clutching her stack of books. Her blue-and-silver prayer book on the top glittered in the sunlight.

I forced myself to let go of Mama, but I didn't run down the apartment stairs leading outside as I usually did, skipping every third step. Instead I trudged slowly down. My feet felt as heavy as my stomach.

"Come on!" Miriam said when she saw me. "You look so pale!"

"Did you get the visas?" I asked. I'd had to head home yesterday before Miriam and her mother had reached the front of the line.

A faint cloud rolled across Miriam's face. "No, not this time," she said. "They shut down the line after fifty people. Then everyone was trying to get visas for anywhere: Australia, China, Argentina."

She tossed her head. "Mother will figure something out! She always does. And if she doesn't, well then I can stay here with you."

"Of course you can," I said. "But why did they shut down the line? People were so desperate! I can't believe they only had fifty spots."

I remembered all those scared faces and wanted to run down to the consulate right then and order the officials to give everyone visas.

"There's more," Miriam said. "I heard Leo Klaus when I came outside this morning. He didn't know I was listening. He said there's violence planned for tonight. Goebbels is stirring up the Nazis."

"Violence? What kind of violence?"

Miriam shook her head. "I don't know. Mama's scared. She said we have to stay inside tonight."

"Papa keeps saying it won't get any worse," I said. "But I'm not sure I believe that. Look at

what's been happening! I think he just *wants* that
to be true."

Miriam didn't say anything in reply, just linked
arms with me. As we came up to the school door,
I felt her grip tighten painfully. It took me a minute
to see why.

The door, which normally stood open, was
closed. There was a sign on it—a big white sign
with black letters—that read: *Every student who is
Jewish or partly Jewish must immediately report to
the headmaster.*

I looked around. The other students stood in
little knots on the pavement, whispering and staring
at us. My face was hot. I felt as if I'd been slapped,
even though I hadn't done anything wrong. But I felt
wrong. I felt gross and stupid.

"What's going on here?" I asked the group
nearest me. Everyone stared at the ground. "Answer
me!" I said.

No one said a thing.

I grabbed for Miriam's hand, looking straight ahead, and together we pushed our way past the others to the headmaster's office. A group of students was already there. I saw Isaac and the Jewish kids in the other grades. Herr Klein was wiping his forehead with a big white handkerchief, the way he always did when he was upset.

"I'm so sorry, students," he said. "The SA came first thing this morning and posted the sign on the door. It's a new law. Jews and Aryans are not to go to school together anymore."

We were silent, digesting this.

"Where are we supposed to go?" Isaac asked after a long time.

Herr Klein didn't look at us. He was rearranging papers on his desk. "You're to go to Frau Schmidt's house. She will hold a school for the Jewish children each day."

I knew Frau Schmidt. She had been the mathematics teacher at school before she retired last year. She lived near the tram depot.

"Why?" I said. "Why do *we* have to leave?" I stood straight and tall and tried to look Herr Klein in the eye.

He didn't meet my gaze. "It's orders," he mumbled.

I didn't know what else to do. It seemed there was nothing else to say. I'd been going to this school since I was six years old. It was as familiar to me as my own hand. But now I was being told to leave.

Silently we walked back to our classroom. I could sense the eyes of the other students boring into me as I gathered my papers from my desk. It was as if Miriam, Isaac, and I had been stamped with a big *JUDE* sign on our foreheads. I felt dirty and ashamed, but I forced myself to look back at them anyway. I had nothing to be ashamed of.

Ten minutes after I'd first arrived at school, I found myself back outside on the sidewalk with the others, about seven of us. I took one last look at the big red-brick building. Then Miriam and I turned our backs and walked away.

We'd gone about six blocks before I realized my bag felt too light. I began rummaging through it as we walked.

"Miriam, I left my mathematics textbook back at school. I'll run back and get it," I said.

"Will they let you in?" she asked.

"I'll ask Herr Klein," I replied. "You go on to Frau Schmidt's with the others, and tell her I'll be along shortly."

"All right," Miriam agreed.

I turned around and began retracing my steps back toward the school. I had just passed the bookstore when I saw a group of boys in the reflection from the glass window. They were following me. Then I heard them: "Jew! Jew! Dirty Jew!"

My heart sped up like a racehorse out of the gate. I kept my head down, took a firmer grip on my books, and walked faster.

"Jewish pig! Jewish pig!" They taunted me through the square.

I glanced at the reflections in the shop windows I passed. There were four or six of them—I didn't turn around long enough to get a good look. But I could see they were all wearing the familiar uniforms of the Hitler Youth boys.

I saw a woman glance at me and hesitate, as if about to stop. Then she hurried on with her bag of groceries.

The boys were getting closer now. But school was still four blocks away. "Jew! Jew!" they shouted.

I whirled around. "Get away!" I shouted back at them.

But they were closing in on me. In an instant, they were so close that I could feel the heat from the bodies behind me. Spittle struck the back of my neck. My breath came in little gasps, and I broke into a run. But it was too late. I felt hands reach out and grab me, jerking me backward. I screamed and wrenched out of their grasp.

The boys clustered around me. Their hair was shaved in the Hitler Youth style—long on the top and short on the sides.

"What should we do with her?" one of them said. He shook my arm hard.

"Get off me!" I yelled. I didn't want them to sense my fear. It was like a hand on my throat, choking me. "Stay away from me!"

One of the boys swiped at me, and I swung my German textbook at him. I connected, hitting him square across the face.

"Pig!" the boy shouted, holding his cheek.

A split second later, rough hands seized me. I struggled and kicked, but there was no release. Their hands were like tight clamps. Then I felt myself being thrown right into the grocer's window.

I tried to scream, but no sound came. I closed my eyes an instant before the crash, my arms up around my head. My body smashed through the glass, and pain flared in my shoulder. Glass flew everywhere—in my eyes, in my mouth, against my skin.

I hit a table covered with potatoes. From behind me, a voice yelled, "Hey! You boys!"

I lay still on the floor, the table partly on top of me, covered in broken glass. Potatoes rolled all over the floor. Everything was silent. The boys must have run away.

"You, girl, are you all right?"

I opened my eyes. The grocer in his canvas apron was brushing glass off my clothes, trying to help me to my feet. "Wait here."

He hurried off and returned with a whisk broom and dustpan. I stood still, trying to breathe as he brushed off my clothing. My shoulder screamed with pain where I had hit the window, and my right arm was bleeding. I brushed at my face, and my hand came away red. My forehead was bleeding too.

"Here, here." The grocer was now binding up my arm with a white towel. He handed me another towel. "Press this against your head." He paused. "I saw what those boys did. That wasn't right."

"No, it wasn't," I managed to say. "The police should arrest them."

But even as I said the words, I knew the SA would never do that. They were on the same side as the boys. Before I knew what was happening, the grocer pushed me out into the street. The boys were gone.

I began stumbling toward home, the gashes on my head and hand beginning to throb. Glass shards prickled me through my clothes. I could hardly take in what had just happened. My skin burned where the boys had grabbed me, as if their hands had been coated in acid.

Mama and Papa, I thought. I had to get home. I had to get there, and then I could rest. Mama would help me. I would lay my head on her lap and let her bind my cuts and change my clothes. Then, maybe then, I could think about what had just happened. Just two blocks. Around the corner and then I would be home.

But I rounded the corner and stopped still. Something was wrong. The square was not full of people walking to work or school like it normally was. Instead, there were Nazis. They were standing in a line around the square, laughing and talking with each other. On the ground in front of them, people were on their knees—men in dark wool hats and long coats.

I looked closer at the people on their knees and saw our next-door neighbor, Meir Dressler, and Papa's friend Herr Goldberg. I saw Isaac's father and the tailor and the janitor from the synagogue. I saw Herr Hochberg, who ran the confectionary shop.

All Jews, I realized.

The men were scrubbing the cobbles. Scrubbing the stones of the square with buckets and brushes. Their faces were grim masks, all of them.

It was a humiliation, I realized. They weren't being hurt—not kicked or punched, at least—but they were being hurt all the same. The SA wanted to make them feel low and small and bad. Just how I'd felt at school.

The knees of the men's trousers were wet. Their hands were wet from the scrub brushes. My chest heaved. Each breath hurt, but whether that was from being thrown through the window or from witnessing the scene in front of me, I couldn't say.

Then I saw Papa. He was in the middle of a row, on his hands and knees, next to Rabbi Gluck. His hat was crooked, and his eyes were down as he scrubbed. Behind him stood a tall, blond, bristly haired Nazi. He was laughing with the Nazi beside him, while Papa scrubbed at his feet.

Rage poured through me. I wanted to run into the crowd and drag Papa away, and at the same time, I wanted to hide my face from his shame. I didn't want to see him brought so low.

That's what they want, I thought. *They* want *us to feel ashamed.* And I did. I did.

But I had to do something.

"Papa!" I whispered, my voice low. I edged forward, keeping an eye on the SA behind my father.

Papa looked up. Our eyes met, and I knew I would never forget the look on his face. It was as if he had suddenly grown old. Old and scared. I had never seen my papa scared before.

Go away! he mouthed, motioning for me to leave.

I shook my head.

Go! Papa motioned at me again, more frantically this time.

I had no choice. I wanted to stay and help—to get Papa out of there—but I didn't want to get him in more trouble. I backed away slowly, away from the shocked, pained expressions of the Jewish men and the excited faces of the young Nazis.

Then I put my head down and ran all the way home.

CHAPTER FOUR

Frankfurt, Germany
Ruth's apartment
November 9, 1938

When I finally walked back into our apartment, Mama's face crumpled at the sight of my wounds. "Ruth!"

I told her about what had happened to me—and what I'd seen in the square. "Mama, I'm going back there! I'll kill them. I'll kill them for what they're doing to us."

"You will not. Hush." Mama's voice was harsh. "Don't cause more trouble than we're already in." She pulled out a large bowl and began bathing my head in warm, soapy water.

Not long after, Papa came in. The knees of his pants were wet. His face was gray. Sitting at the table, I buried my face in my arms. I didn't want to see my papa this way.

"Mendel." Mama paused. "Ruth told me what happened in the square—"

"I don't want to talk about it," Papa interrupted. Then he caught sight of my cuts. "Ruth—what . . . ?" He took my head in his hands, examining my cuts.

"Some Hitler Youth boys attacked her," Mama explained quietly. It was as if just voicing the words hurt her.

Papa didn't say any more after that. The lines in his face deepened as he touched my wounds.

That night, Mama seemed determined to make us have a regular family meal. She cooked the chicken soup silently, her chin squared in a way that made it clear she did not want to talk any more about the events of the afternoon.

But when we were gathered around the table, with the good steam from the soup bathing our faces, Papa cleared his throat. "Today—what happened in the square—"

"Do you still think it won't get worse, Papa?" I interrupted angrily. Why were my parents being so stubborn? "How can you still say that after what happened to me? And to you?"

"I have to believe that, Ruth," Papa said. "I hope this is the end." But his voice was not as sure as it had been before.

"No more talk of this. Let's enjoy supper," Mama said briskly. She smiled, her round face glowing in the soft light. "We're together. That's what's important."

I knew what she was trying to do. I could see it in her eyes. Outside these walls, the world seemed to be flying out of control. We were at the mercy of the SA and those who followed them. But here, in our apartment, Mama could protect us. She could make our world safe and comfortable. So that's what she was going to do.

And we were together. The chicken soup was salty and hot and delicious. The pain in my head and shoulder had finally faded to a dull ache. I looked at my parents seated across the table, their faces bathed in the steam from the bowls, the worn silver candlesticks, the photos of my grandparents on the walls behind us.

My breath caught. Despite what my parents said, all might not go well with us. What had happened on the street today might not be the worst of our troubles, but only the beginning.

I looked at Papa. I suddenly felt I must memorize every detail of his appearance. I stared hard at each line and crevice on his beloved face. It seemed desperately important, but I could not explain why.

After dinner, I took my bath as usual, then went into the living room to kiss my parents goodnight. They were sitting in their usual spots—Mama in her low chair and Papa on the couch—but they weren't knitting and reading as they usually did. They were just sitting.

"Goodnight, Mama. Goodnight, Papa," I said, bending down to peck Mama on the cheek.

She patted my face with her hand. "Goodnight, Ruth."

"Mama, your hand is so cold," I said. I took her hand in mine and rubbed it back and forth to warm it up.

"Never mind," she said. She chafed my hand. "Yours are warm from the bath."

"Ruth," Papa said, "listen to me." His dark eyes were fixed on me with an intensity I'd never seen before. "You are not to go outside tonight. No matter what. If you hear strange noises, I want you to get up out of your bed and hide in the wardrobe in the hallway."

"What? Why, Papa? What noises?" I asked.

"Never mind," Mama cut in. "Obey your papa." She pursed her lips, the way she did when she was upset.

"I will," I said softly.

I bent and kissed them each on the forehead, then turned to leave the room. But when I reached the doorway, something made me turn around. Mama and Papa were both sitting very still, their heads bent. Without looking up, Papa put out his hand, and Mama took it.

I watched them for a long time, but they didn't move. Finally I turned from the doorway, leaving my parents sitting in that strange silence, still holding hands.

In my bed, I pulled the covers up to my chin and squeezed my eyes shut. For an instant, I felt

the Hitler Youth boys' hands on me again, lifting

me. I felt how strong they were, their arms like wiry

bands. They could have done anything, I knew, and

no one would have stopped them.

CHAPTER FIVE

Frankfurt, Germany
Ruth's apartment
November 9, 1938

I awoke from the black tunnel of sleep with a start, my heart hammering.

"Hurry, Ruth," Mama was whispering, leaning over me. She held out my bathrobe.

"What?" I rubbed my eyes.

"Shhh!" Mama's breath was hot on my cheek, and her hands shook as she draped the bathrobe around my shoulders.

Papa stood at the window. He drew the curtain aside, watching something down on the street below. Suddenly he sucked in a breath and dropped the curtain as if it had turned into a snake about to strike.

"Get in the wardrobe," he said, pushing Mama and me ahead of him. "Hurry, they're coming."

"Who?" I clung to Mama.

"Hush!" Mama's voice was harsh. I'd never heard her speak that way before.

Papa hurried us from the room toward the wardrobe in the hall. The floorboards were slick and icy under my feet. Then I saw it—a weird orange light patterning the walls.

Wrestling free of Papa's grasp, I darted to the window and gasped. Frankfurt's two huge synagogues—the same synagogues I'd seen every morning and every evening of my life from this very window—were burning.

Even from here I could hear the crackle of the flames and smell the smoke. The building was black against the light inside it. It often looked that way on Sabbath evenings. I'd always loved the light, pouring through the stained glass onto the snow. But this light was different, frantic. It seemed to be devouring the synagogue from the inside out.

People were everywhere on the street, dark figures lit by the hideous light from the fires. They were breaking the windows of all the shops and apartment windows. I saw our across-the-square neighbor, Herr Korn, a Gentile, smashing the window of the tailor shop. The policemen were everywhere, but they were just standing and watching, doing nothing to stop the destruction.

Then I saw next door. Rabbi Gluck, Miriam's father, was being dragged down his front stoop by two SA men.

Terror flooded me. "Oh, what will they do to him? Where is Miriam?" I whisper-screamed.

Mama moved to the window and clutched me to her. Outside, we saw one SA man pull Rabbi

Gluck's head back. The other soldier took a large pair of scissors from his pocket and cut off Rabbi's Gluck's beard. Then they released him, shoving the rabbi down the stoop so that he stumbled and fell on his hands and knees. One of the SA men kicked him in the stomach over and over.

"Rabbi Gluck!" Tears were pouring down my face. I couldn't bear to see them beating him. I struggled to free myself from my mother's grasp. "Let me go! We have to help him! I have to get down there! We need to bring him inside!"

Mama didn't answer. She just pulled me tighter against her, pressing my face to her chest. I could hear her heart hammering like a pounding horse.

Just then a huge crash sounded from outside. I wrenched away from Mama and stared down at the street. A mob had pushed over one of the telephone poles. Then, all together, they picked it up and turned toward our apartment building.

Another crash shook the walls. They were using the pole like a battering ram to break down the door.

"Hide, Ruth!" Papa grabbed my arm so hard I cried out. He propelled me down the hall and shoved me into the wardrobe, pushing me against my mother. Then he slammed the door, as if closing our coffin lid.

I huddled against Mama in the darkness. I could feel her silently praying into the back of my neck.

From outside I could hear the voices. Many voices, shouting. They were getting closer. Then a tremendous crash shook the house. They had broken in the door. They were coming up the stairs.

I crammed my fist into my mouth to keep from screaming. Mama shook against me. All I could think was, *Papa is out there.*

Mama clamped her hand over my mouth, and I heard boots pounding up the stairs.

"Where's the rabbi?" a man's voice shouted.

"He's not here! You've got the wrong apartment!" Papa shouted back. It sounded as if he was standing at the head of the stairs.

"Move out of the way, Jew!" another man shouted. "Your kind doesn't deserve to live near Aryans."

From inside the wardrobe I heard a collision, followed by a thud and the sounds of Papa groaning.

"They're hurting him, Mama," I whispered into my fist. I wanted to get out there and help him, but Mama held me so tightly I could barely breathe, let alone move. I could hear the air sobbing in and out of her chest, tiny breaths of terror.

A moment later, the apartment was filled with animal-like grunts and thuds and stampings. They were rampaging through our home, overturning furniture. Glass smashed and tinkled. They must have broken the windows, I realized, because suddenly, the shouting and screaming out on the street was much louder.

It felt as if I spent a year in that wardrobe, crouched against Mama, our bodies aching. All I knew was that no matter what, they must not find us.

Finally, finally, the boots receded. The noises around us faded. The only sounds were from the street.

Mama pushed the door open a crack and peeked out. A cold draft blew into the wardrobe. "Mendel!" she gasped and scrambled out.

I followed, almost falling on my cramped legs. Papa lay against the wall, his nose bleeding and his eyes already puffing up. They must have hit him in the face.

"I'm all right," he groaned, hoisting himself up. "Stop, Gitla."

The apartment was completely ransacked. All our furniture had been overturned. The living room was a sea of broken china and torn pages from books. Every window had been broken, and I shivered as the cold November wind swept in.

The noise from the street was louder than ever. Women were screaming, and men were shouting and moaning in the square below. I heard a huge crashing and cracking that must have been part of the burning synagogues collapsing.

Numbly, I bent down and picked up a crumpled page at my feet. It was the title page from *Little Women*. Mama and Papa had given it to me on my ninth birthday.

To our Ruth, Papa had written. *Our hope is that you will become a strong woman like Jo. Love, Papa and Mama.*

I curled my fingers around the paper and stuffed it in my pocket. "Papa, please," I begged. "What will they do to Rabbi Gluck? Where is Miriam?"

Mama was crouched on the floor, pressing a handkerchief to Papa's nose.

"I don't know," Papa said. His voice sounded like a sleepwalker's. "Rabbi Gluck has likely been arrested."

"Arrested? Why? He hasn't done anything! We have to go find him!" I pulled at Mama's arm, trying to lift her to her feet.

"Stop it, Ruth! Do you think we can get him back from the SA? You cannot fight them!" Mama cried.

"I'm going to try!" I shouted back, my hands balled into fists. "Someone has to!" I was sobbing now. I wanted to wake up, but this wasn't a nightmare. It was real.

Then, from downstairs, we heard voices: "SA! Get out into the square!"

CHAPTER SIX

Mama and I stared at each other. Mama's eyes were huge. She seemed frozen with fear. I couldn't move.

"Do everything they say," Papa ordered. He grabbed our coats from the wardrobe and slung them around our shoulders just as heavy boots pounded up the stairs.

Two SA officers in brown uniforms burst into the room. "Put some clothes on and come with us," one ordered. "All Jews arc to report to the square."

My fingers were shaking so badly I couldn't fasten my coat. Mama grabbed my elbow, hard, and pressed me close to her side as we followed the officers out of the room.

Swirling soot struck me in the face as soon as we stepped outside. I coughed and wiped at my face. Smoke hung everywhere. I could hear the roar and crackle of the synagogues burning and people crying and shouting and screaming. Every few moments, glass shattered.

The square was full of people, all pressed together. Thousands of Jews—men, women, children. A soldier near us stood over an old man with a gray beard, hitting him with a stick. The old man was screaming as he lay curled up on the ground, his hands over his head. A few feet away, a woman who must have been his wife was sobbing, her arms around two little children. They were crying too and hiding their faces in her coat.

My eyes stung with the soot from the fire, and I wiped at my face over and over. Then I heard Mama scream, "No, no, no, Mendel!"

I turned and saw that an SA soldier was dragging my father away by the arm. "Get with the other men!" the soldier shouted.

Papa was fighting back, pulling away. In response, the soldier punched him in the jaw.

"Papa!" I screamed, trying to reach him. He was crumpled on the ground, holding his face.

Mama held my sleeve in a tight grip. Just then a huge crash came from the burning synagogue, and soldiers' voices shouted. The SA officer gave Papa one last shove and hurried away.

I rushed over to where my father lay. "Are you hurt?" I asked, wrapping my arm around his shoulders.

Papa raised his face, and I gasped. The lower half of his face was already puffy and black and blue. He tried to say something, but his voice came out in a mumble.

"I think his jaw is broken," Mama said.

"We have to get him to a doctor," I said.

Mama looked around at the mass of people around us. "How will we get a doctor? The doctors are out here too!"

"We have to at least try!" I said. "He needs help. Maybe we can slip away without the SA noticing." I tried to lift Papa but stumbled on the wet cobblestones and fell against him. "Mama, you have to help me."

"Ruth!" someone cried just then.

I turned. It was Miriam and her mother with the other women from their building. Her father was nowhere to be seen.

"Miriam!" I raced toward her and clung to my friend. "Mrs. Gluck! Help us, please! Papa is badly hurt."

Miriam's eyes were huge in the orange light.

"Ruth, what is happening?" she almost whispered.

"Why are they doing this?"

I hugged my friend as tightly as I could. She was something familiar in a night where the world seemed to have exploded. Mrs. Gluck and Mama were struggling to get Papa to his feet. Miriam and I joined our mothers, and together we hoisted him to his feet.

Papa barely seemed able to walk. I could tell he was in terrible pain. His face was white and dripping sweat.

"Oh no, oh no," Mrs. Gluck moaned.

I had thought this night couldn't get any worse. But when I followed her gaze and saw a group of SA soldiers pushing through the crowd, I realized it was about to.

CHAPTER **SEVEN**

The soldiers were carrying the Torah scrolls from the synagogue. They threw them into a huge pile on the cobblestones. Other people added armloads of prayer books.

They must have taken them from the synagogue before they set fire to the building, I realized.

I heard moaning from the crowd of Jewish men being guarded by a ring of SA. Other people were shouting encouragement. "Burn them! Burn them!"

A man pushed through the crowd with a flaming stick in his hand. He flung it on the pile of Torahs and prayer books. The old, dry paper ignited almost immediately. I watched the licking flames consume the Torah.

"No! No!" Mrs. Gluck rushed forward.

An SA soldier flung an arm out in her way. "Stay back, Jew," he said, catching her full in the chest.

Mrs. Gluck fell back against us, sobbing, clawing to try to get to the fire. People stood around the flames, guarding it, keeping the Jewish men in the crowd from rushing at the fire. Then I saw Rabbi Gluck. I almost didn't recognize him. His face looked strange without his chest-length black beard, and his hat had been knocked off. He was kneeling at the side of the fire. At first I thought he was praying. But Jews don't kneel to pray.

Then I saw the two SA officers standing on either side. They were holding his arms. They were forcing him to watch the fire, I realized.

"Miriam!" I whispered. I couldn't make my voice any louder.

But Miriam didn't hear me. She was crouching
over her mother, who was now lying on the ground.
Mama and Papa didn't see Rabbi Gluck either. No
one saw but me.

As I watched, the SA officers let go of Rabbi
Gluck's arms. He fell to his face on the stones.

It was as if he didn't have the strength in his body
to stay up. He lay there, face down, until an officer
dragged him into the crowd by his ankles. Then he
was gone.

I had a secret now, I realized. I couldn't tell
Miriam or her mother. I couldn't tell them how

I had seen Rabbi Gluck—a father and husband and leader of our community—lying sobbing on the dirty cobbles as the Torah burned inches from his face.

The fire was huge now. People were dragging pews from the synagogues over and piling them on. The crackling and snapping of the flames filled the air. Other people were pulling furniture from the open doors of the apartments—tables and chairs, beds, mattresses, armloads of clothes and books— and throwing them on the fire.

"Ruth! Hurry!" Mama was motioning me from the edge of the square. "Dr. Berman thinks he can help Papa if we can make it to his office. Come!"

"Mama, I can't leave Miriam!" I looked back at my best friend. Mrs. Gluck was on her feet now, leaning against the side of a building.

"Ruth, come!" Mama's face looked frantic. "Dr. Berman will not wait!" I spotted the doctor at the edge of the square, motioning us.

"No!" I hissed. "You go. I'll wait here! I'll be here when you return."

Mama looked from Papa to me and back again. "Stay exactly where you are," she finally said, her voice cracking with agony. "Don't move even one inch." She gave me a final, desperate look and dragged my father away. He stumbled by her side, his long frame bent and his hand clamped over the side of his face.

I ran over to Miriam and grabbed her. We clung to each other. My face and hands were black and sticky from the soot, and we were shaking, we were so chilled through.

How will I find them again? I thought. But I pushed the thought away. I would find them again because I had to. I had to keep Miriam and myself safe. I had to survive. This night would end. It just had to.

CHAPTER EIGHT

Suddenly Miriam grasped my arm so hard, I cried out. "Oh, Ruth! Ruth!" She pointed.

I followed her finger. "Quick!" I said. "Don't let your mother see!"

But it was too late.

"Oh, our things! Those are our things!" wailed Mrs. Gluck.

A mob was shouting and tugging and yanking the furniture out of Miriam's apartment. I saw their dining table, where I had eaten too many Shabbos meals to count. I saw Miriam's carved wooden bed with the white canopy, dragging and broken.

"Stay back!" the SA soldier yelled.

Beside him, I saw the civil policemen from our district. They were all just standing there, watching, doing nothing. I knew those men. I'd known them since I was born. And they were just observing, as if they had no power. Or had all the power. They surrounded the fire, keeping their backs to it, facing the crowd with their sticks drawn. No one could touch it to put it out.

Rage boiled up in me as people crowded around, grabbing things to throw on the fire. The mob was still dragging furniture and clothes out the doorway. People were shoving now, pushing forward, and I held on to Miriam. I couldn't see her mother anymore—she had been swallowed up in the crowd.

"Oh, my clothes!" Miriam was sobbing. "My dolls!" People were tossing armloads of things onto the blaze, making the flames flare up clear and yellow in the night. Miriam gasped. "My books!"

They were throwing books on now, flinging them on with abandon. I saw the leather covers curling and crisping. Half-burnt pages flew up into the night sky, surrounded by sparks.

The crowd was yelling now, cheering on those who were dumping the books onto the flames. Through the smoke, I saw Frau Hermann. It was impossible to believe that it had been just the other day that she'd warned us about the trouble coming. Her face was so filled with rage that I barely recognized her.

I coughed and coughed, nausea boiling up in me. The smoke was choking me and filling my eyes. I had to get away from here. I had to rest. Miriam's weight against me dragged me down. I couldn't hold her up anymore. I wanted my own bed, in my own clean room, with my own white sheets.

"Ruth! Ruth, my prayer book!" Miriam's desperate voice brought me back.

I swam up through layers of smoke until I could focus my eyes again. The little blue-and-silver book—Miriam's most treasured possession—was lying on the edge of the fire. She'd carried it to every Shabbos service since she was six years old. We'd held those pages together, each with a side, standing next to each other as we prayed.

"No!" I screamed. A blond SA soldier looked at me, right into my face. His eyes were empty. "No, they won't have it!"

I ran forward, but Miriam caught my arm. "Ruth! What are you doing?"

"They won't have it!" I struggled to get free from her grasp. "I'll get it, let me go."

"Stop! They'll beat you!" Miriam whispered.

But I could barely hear her. My rage blotted out everything else.

I yanked my arm free and darted into the crowd. The fire was like a raging monster, chewing through the books furiously. All the hate and rage from the crowd seemed to be fueling those flames.

Miriam's prayer book was lying just out of reach of the blaze. It was on the cobblestones, but I knew the edges would catch fire as soon as the books next to it were set aflame.

I reached into my pocket and pulled out a scarf. I tied it over my head and drew it close to conceal my features as best I could. I buttoned my coat up to my neck to cover my nightgown. Then, as softly as I could, I wiggled my way past one person watching the fire, then another. Finally, hiding behind a large woman standing right in front of the fire—and the prayer book—I peeked around her side.

The SA soldiers were standing with their sticks in their hands, surveying the crowd. Occasionally, someone would burst through the crowd and throw another armload of books on. I heard moaning and sobbing from the Jews watching.

If I could just dart out and grab the book, I could disappear into the crowd before anyone caught me—I hoped. I was small and quick. Perhaps the element of surprise would give me a few extra seconds. No one would think a twelve-year-old girl would disobey SA soldiers. If I just waited until they were distracted . . . and until the wind brought the smoke near me. That would provide a moment of cover.

Behind my human wall, I waited. My heart was pounding in my ears. I kept my eyes fixed on the prayer book. Then, a huge crash echoed across the square. One of the burning synagogue walls had collapsed. Every head turned to look. That was my chance.

Darting out from behind the huge woman, I ran toward the fire. I felt horribly exposed, like a rabbit in a field of hunters. "There, get her!" someone shouted.

CHAPTER NINE

I sobbed under my breath. Then the smoke, the blessed smoke, rolled over me, offering cover. Coughing and choking, I fumbled toward where I thought the prayer book lay.

The heat from the flames battered my face as I grabbed at the shapes on the ground. Then I felt it—the embossed silver and leather cover of Miriam's book. I knew it like my own face.

I grabbed at it, sliding it toward me as the crowd thrashed and heaved behind me. Flames were licking at the edges of the book. Unthinking,

I beat them out with my bare hands. Then, gasping for breath, I crawled backward.

"You! What are you doing?" a man's voice shouted from the crowd.

I didn't wait to see if it was an SA officer or a civilian. I squeezed myself into the mass of people and stuffed the prayer book under my coat.

"Oh, Ruth!" Miriam cried when I finally found her again. I handed her the prayer book, and she clutched it to her chest. Tears ran down her filthy cheeks, leaving black tracks. "Thank you."

"Where's your mother?" I asked. "Have you seen Mama or Papa?"

Miriam shook her head. "I don't know where anyone is," she whispered.

"Let's try to get back to my apartment. We can wait for the others there," I said.

If they ever come home, a voice said quietly in my head. I shoved that voice away, grasped Miriam by the hand, and slipped through the crowd. I kept my head down, trying to look invisible.

No one stopped us—perhaps because we had no adult men with us—and we found the door of my apartment building gaping open like a black hole. The cold wind whistled up the staircase. An eerie silence filled my ears after the shouting on the square.

Upstairs, the rooms were dark, cold, and silent. Soot wafted in on the wind blowing in through the open windows. Books and papers lay in torn heaps on the floor. Our kitchen table lay overturned against a wall. The floor was thick with broken crockery. In Mama and Papa's room, the wardrobe door gaped open. Mama's clothes were tossed in a blackened pile. Someone must have tried to set them on fire, but the fire had gone out.

Miriam and I crunched over the debris-covered floor and lay down on my bed, clutching each other,

listening to the screams and shouts from the square.
Sometime before dawn, we fell asleep.

―――――――――――――――――――

We woke in the cold, gray light of day, and I
pushed myself upright. My entire body ached, and
my mouth was so dry I had to unstick my tongue
from the roof of my mouth. I rubbed my eyes. My
fists came away black.

Miriam was still sleeping deeply, her hair tangled
across her face, her coat wrapped around her. I eased
myself out of bed and picked my way over to the
broken window. The fires still burned, pale now in
the dawn light. The square was full of men being
guarded by the SA, and the streets were full of men
shouting. It seemed incredible to me that the mobs
wouldn't have gone home when daylight came.

I peered through the window, trying to spot
Papa, not knowing if I wanted to. I couldn't see him,
though, and I was afraid someone would spot me

at the window. I turned away and crept along the debris-strewn hallway until I reached the kitchen.

When I saw Mama and Papa sitting at the table, their faces pale with fatigue, I almost wept with joy. They were drinking coffee but no milk. The milk had been emptied all over the floor, along with the rest of the contents of our icebox. Papa's face was horribly swollen with purple bruises all along his jaw.

"Mama, Papa!" I cried and rushed at them.

"Thank God you're safe." Mama pressed my head against her shoulder, pulling me onto her lap.

I let myself be held for a moment, then pulled free. "Papa, why aren't you down below with the other men?" I asked.

Papa shook his head. "They started rounding up the men before dawn, I hear. Your mother and I managed to slip past them in the dark."

All the fear I'd been holding back all night—it boiled up. "Papa, all our things, our windows, they're broken! And poor Miriam! They pushed Mrs. Gluck, and they were beating Rabbi Gluck, and the fire, the synagogues! What's happening?" I clung to Mama as the words poured from my mouth and tears poured down my cheeks.

"Where's Mama?" a small voice came from the doorway. Miriam stood there, one of my blankets wrapped around her shoulders. Soot and tears had dried on her face like a dirty mask.

"Miriam, bubbeleh, come sit down." Mama got up from her own chair. "Come here, I'll make you tea."

Miriam perched on the very edge of one of the chairs as if it might jump up and hit her. "Mrs. Bloch, where's Mama?" she asked again.

I scooted my chair closer and put one arm over Miriam's shoulders, trying to comfort her. But she shook it off.

"Do you know where my father is?" Her voice rose higher and higher with each word.

"He's probably down the square, if he's anywhere," Papa said gently. "Your apartment's deserted. We don't know where your mother is. I'm sorry."

Miriam stood up, my blanket falling to the floor around her. "I have to find my mother!" She rushed to the doorway and looked around wildly.

I jumped up and caught her arm. "Stop, Miriam!" I said. "The streets aren't safe—the mobs are still out there."

"I have to!" Miriam cried, struggling like a bird in a trap. "I have to find Mama! Let me go!"

"Sit down!" Mama jumped up and pushed Miriam into a chair. "You'll bring the SA down on us if you keep it up."

I froze, my mouth open. I'd never heard Mama use that voice or push anyone anywhere. The kitchen was silent then, except for the sound of Miriam's gasping sobs.

Finally I said, "I'll go find her." I had evaded the SA last night. I'd have to do it again. I grabbed my sweater hanging from its hook on the wall.

"No!" Mama said. "Ruth, they'll see you! We don't know what the SA will do!"

I kept my eyes on Miriam. "I'll find her, OK?" I repeated. "Just stay inside."

"No!" Papa stood up. "I will go. Sit down, Ruth." He pushed me into a chair. I fell back, stunned.

"Mendel!" Mama wailed, but Papa didn't even look at her. He took his hat from the wall and left, closing the door behind him.

Miriam and I rushed to the window in my room just in time to see Papa appear from the doorway below. He strode onto the square, but he hadn't gone twenty steps before two SA soldiers grabbed him from either side.

"Get in line!" I could just make out one saying. "All Jews are under arrest." They shoved him toward a group of men standing at the edge of the square nearest our apartment.

"No!" Mama came up behind us and peered out the window too. "No! They're going to take him away!"

Cold fear seized me. "Papa!" I called through the open window. "Papa!"

It was too noisy down below for anyone to hear me. The SA were barking at the men and gesturing with their weapons.

They were ordering the men to unlace their shoes, I realized. Only Papa wasn't bending over like the rest. He was standing straight up, staring defiantly ahead. An SA officer barked at him, swung his weapon in a gesture.

"Oh, what is he doing?" Mama whispered frantically. "Do as they say! Do as they say!"

But Papa shook his head and stared straight ahead. Another man shuffled up to the SA officer and handed over a handful of black shoelaces. Only Papa's shoes remained neatly tied.

Groups of men were being marched from the crowded square with SA guards on either side. The SA officers guarding Papa's group shouted something and swung their weapons, gesturing at the other groups leaving. *Move out,* they were ordering.

The other men in the group turned and started following one of the guards. Their faces all bore the same tight fear. But Papa clenched his jaw and stared out over the ruins of the two great synagogues.

As I watched in horror, one of the guards stepped forward. With a crack I could clearly hear, the guard struck Papa across the face with his weapon.

"Papa!" I screamed, not caring who heard me.

"No!" Mama shrieked. She lunged forward toward the window. For an instant, I thought she would fall out. Then Miriam and I grabbed her, pulling her back.

"Papa, Papa!" I cried, holding on to Mama.

"I'm coming!" I had to get down there.

Papa was on the ground now, his body curled up as the SA guards surrounded him, kicking him in his stomach, back, and head. I could hear the grunts of the guards, but no one stepped forward to help my father. The other Jewish men huddled together, turning their faces away.

"No, no, no," Mama moaned.

I wondered if I would vomit. I thought of Papa's already bruised face. On the other side of Mama, Miriam's face was gray. She clung to Mama's sleeve as if it were the only thing that mattered in the world.

I couldn't stay up there one more second.

"I'm going down there."

Mama didn't seem to hear me. It was as if she was in another world. Miriam nodded and helped Mama slide to the floor.

I ran from the room and down the apartment steps, skidding on the ash and papers covering everything. I clung to the banister to keep from falling and burst out into the square. Papa was just a few yards ahead of me.

"Papa!" I screamed. "I'm coming!" I ran forward as if the SA guarding him were nothing but puppies.

Papa looked up through the mask of blood covering his face. "Ruth, no!" I heard him say.

Before I could react, two SA lifted me off the ground, their hard hands clamped over my arms. They slung me back against a nearby bench. "Get away," one of the soldiers growled. He pointed his rifle at my head.

Slowly, not taking my eyes off the barrel of the gun, I scrambled to my feet and backed away. The SA turned and barked an order. Two of the guards yanked Papa to his feet. He didn't seem to be able

to stand on his own. They dragged him over to a
nearby truck and heaved him into the back as if he
were a sack of potatoes. Then they slammed the
black doors, and the truck drove from the square.

CHAPTER TEN

In the cold, gray light, Mrs. Gluck smoothed a paper across her knees. "The men have been taken to concentration camps, Gitla," she said. "They may be released. Or they may not. But either way, the girls must get out."

Miriam sat close to her mother, where she'd been since Mrs. Gluck had shown up at our door late the night before. Mrs. Gluck had found refuge in the rubble of the synagogue and hadn't dared move until the mobs on the street finally dispersed.

"Jewish children can register for this," Mrs. Gluck continued. She held the paper at arm's length. "Kindertransport. It's a train to England. But no parents or any adults. Only children."

Leave without Mama? I thought. *With Papa who knows where, in some camp?* I couldn't imagine it.

I felt as alone and directionless as a dead leaf carried across the square in the wind. But I also knew I couldn't stay here.

Mama nodded slowly. "They must get out," she agreed. But she sounded uncertain. All her determination seemed to have drained away.

Mrs. Gluck stood up. "We'll go to the transport office right away, see if we can get them places."

Our mothers were gone for two hours. When they returned, we only needed one look at their faces to tell us that not all the news was good.

"Ruth, you have a place on the transport," Mama said. She glanced at Mrs. Gluck.

Mrs. Gluck looked at Miriam. "I was behind Gitla in line." She seemed to force the words out. "I'm sorry, Miriam. The transport is full."

We stood silently, taking in the news. Miriam and I looked at our mothers' faces, then at each other. I didn't want to leave my friend behind—or my mother. But one look at Mama's face told me I would be going.

"But I'll come back, won't I, Mama?" I finally asked. "We'll see each other again."

"Of course," Mama said. "It's just temporary."

———————

Mama and I had three weeks to pack and prepare. There was still no word from Papa. I tried to see Miriam whenever I could, but there was tension between us now that I didn't know how to fix. Our lives had always been entwined. Now the strands were separating.

Mama stitched my name on every piece of clothing she packed for me. She always slept with a little pillow on her bed, on top of her big pillow, and one day, as we were putting clothes in my suitcase, she gave it to me. It smelled like her, and I pushed it into the suitcase among my skirts and blouses.

The night before I was to leave, a knock came at the door. Miriam stood there on the landing. For a long moment, we just looked at each other.

"You're leaving in the morning?" she finally asked.

I nodded. I felt awkward, as if I were going to a party she wasn't invited to. I suddenly thought of my birthday, just a month ago, when Miriam had stood at this door in her best green dress, ready for my party. She'd been with me when no one else had wanted to come to my party. But now I couldn't be with her. I couldn't stand with her the way she'd always stood with me.

"The train leaves at nine o'clock."

Miriam nodded. Then suddenly, she pulled something out from under her coat and thrust it at me. It was her blue-and-silver prayer book—the one I'd rescued from the fire. The edges were singed brown-black now.

"Here. I want you to take this to England," she said.

"What? Why?" I asked.

"To remember me," she said. She pushed it into my hand.

"I'm coming back, you know," I reminded her. "I'll see you again."

"Just to remember me while you're gone, then," Miriam said. "Until you come back." Two tiny tears suddenly glittered at the edges of her eyes.

I threw my arms around her neck and hugged her hard. "I will take care of it," I whispered. "And I will come back."

The next morning, Mama and I walked onto the platform where I was to board the Kindertransport. Parents and children surrounded us in a confused jumble. A woman in a tweed suit was calling instructions I couldn't hear over the hiss and puff of the steam engine waiting at the platform edge.

Someone put a yellow ticket around my neck. *57,* it read. Someone else wired another matching ticket to my suitcase.

All around me, parents were sobbing. I saw small children clinging to their mothers' hands. Older children, closer to my age, were climbing up onto the train carriage. I looked up at Mama. Her face was twisted with grief I had never seen before.

"Board!" the conductor called.

"Mama," I tried to say, but my throat was so dry it came out like a croak.

Mama bent down and pressed my head against her chest. I felt her lips in my hair. She pulled back and looked into my face as if she were trying to drink it in.

"We'll be together soon," she whispered. Her face contorted for an instant. Then she was pushing me toward the train. "Go, go!" she said.

I scrambled up the carriage steps and looked back. Mama's head was bowed, and her shoulders were shaking. The train shook and puffs of steam billowed out over the platform. I ran into the nearest compartment and thrust my head and shoulders out the window. My mother was right below, reaching her hand up. Other parents pressed in around her, each trying to reach their own child's hand.

I reached down and touched my mother's fingers. "I'll be back, Mama!" I cried.

"I'll be here, darling!" she called back. "I'll always be here waiting for you." Her voice was

thick and her face wet with tears, but she was trying to smile.

The train began to move, slowly at first, then picking up speed. My mother ran along the platform, pushing through the crowd, waving to me. I twisted around to see one last glimpse of her, and then the station fell behind us.

Facing forward, I clasped my hands in my lap and stared straight ahead. Everything I'd ever known was behind me—my parents, Miriam, my bedroom, my city.

I wanted to hurl myself off the train and run back to my old life as fast as I could. I wanted to feel my mother's arms around me. I wanted to walk to school with my best friend. I wanted to feel the cobbles I knew as well as the walls of my own room.

As I sat there, on the train carrying me into an unknown future, I realized I didn't know if I would ever do that again. But I would have to be strong, no matter what. I had no one to rely on now. I did not know my place in this new world, and my old world was gone, at least for now.

If I was going to an orphanage, or a family, or somewhere else, I would take care of myself. I would remember Mama and Papa. I would pray, and I would write letters every day. And when I came back, I would never leave them again.

I forced myself to stay in my seat, holding tight to the silver-and-blue prayer book in my lap. I didn't know what lay ahead of me. I didn't know a single face at the other end of my journey. I didn't know where I would sleep that night, or the night after, or the night after that.

But I knew I would survive. I hadn't fought back against the SA to give up now. I owed that to my family and my friends. To the ones I'd left behind and prayed I'd see again.

A NOTE FROM THE AUTHOR

When I set out to write Ruth's story, I struggled.
This was a story about survival and fighting against
an entire system. What was one young girl going to
do against the entire Nazi regime? That feeling of
helplessness against the system is something a lot of
Holocaust survivors remember feeling. I didn't want to
ignore that, or pretend that Ruth and her family were
somehow going to stop the horrific events to come.

But then I realized a solution of sorts—I needed to
focus on the small acts of resistance. *Think small,* I told
myself. *Think daily life, not world events.*

Ruth could fight against the injustices she saw at
every turn. Others—real-life survivors—did the same.
Even in the concentration camps, survivors remember
those who refused to give in—those who resisted.

The story of the Holocaust is a long one, but
Kristallnacht, or Night of Broken Glass, is a beginning
of sorts. It began on the evening of November 9, 1938,
and continued through November 10, 1938, in Germany,
Austria, and a place called Sudetenland.

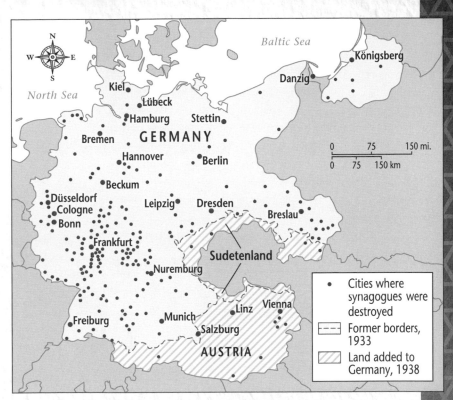

Kristallnacht was a violent pogrom that took place beginning on the night of November 9, 1938, and continuing through the following day. Nearly 300 synagogues were burned or destroyed.

This night of violence and vandalism was the first time the Nazis used violence against Jews. Anti-Jewish mobs smashed the windows of Jewish shops and homes. So many windows were smashed that the streets were littered with broken glass. The mobs tore up cemeteries and burned 267 synagogues. More than 7,500 Jewish businesses were vandalized, robbed, and looted.

The mobs also physically beat—and in at least one hundred cases, killed—Jewish people. The SA (Hitler's storm troopers) and Hitler Youth also took part in the violence. Some wore civilian clothes to hide their involvement.

More than thirty thousand Jewish men were arrested during the night and day of Kristallnacht. They were taken to the Dachau and Buchenwald concentration camps, among others. Most were released and encouraged to leave Germany.

The man behind Kristallnacht was Joseph Goebbels, Hitler's propaganda minister. Goebbels was responsible for controlling the German press and distributing information in support of the Nazis and against the Jews.

Goebbels used the death of Ernst vom Rath, a German diplomat, as an excuse to call for mass violence against Jews across Germany. (Vom Rath was shot and killed by Herschel Grynszpan, a seventeen-year-old Polish boy, in Paris, France, on November 7, 1938.) Goebbels, however, presented Kristallnacht as a spontaneous uprising against Jews by the German people.

The Boemestrasse Synagogue in Frankfurt, Germany, was burned during Kristallnacht, also known as Night of Broken Glass.

The German government declared Jews themselves responsible for the destruction. They imposed a one billion Reichsmark fine ($400 million in 1938) on the Jews of Germany.

Many Jews fled Germany after Kristallnacht. Some children were able to secure places in the Kindertransport, a program that took Jewish children from Germany to England, mostly by train.

On September 1, 1939, ten months after Kristallnacht, Germany invaded Poland. The Kindertransports mostly ended, although a few continued until 1940. Most of the children sent to England never saw their parents again. People believed that when the trains pulled away, it would be only a matter of time until they were reunited. But tragically, many of the parents left behind were killed by the Nazis.

As a Jewish person, I knew some things about Kristallnacht. I remember learning about it in Hebrew school and being completely bored. But I wasn't bored when I set out to research this story. Instead, I was fascinated by the fear, chaos, and bravery of that period.

When I set out to do the research for this story, I read many first-person accounts from survivors. I especially drew upon the documentary *Into the Arms of Strangers,* directed by Mark Jonathan Harris, which aired in 2000.

I watched carefully and took many notes. Then I incorporated as many true experiences into this book as I could. This was a fictional story, so Ruth was my own creation. But I wanted her to embody as many real memories and experiences of survivors as possible.

Ruth getting thrown through the window by the Hitler Youth boys is a true story, although that survivor was a boy. Ruth feeling that she needed to memorize her parents' faces at dinner the night of Kristallnacht is also a real survivor's memory.

The birthday party no one comes to, the children being shut out of school, Papa's belief that the worst had already happened, the lines at the consulate, the burning of the Frankfurt synagogues, the scene at the train station . . . all these and more are real survivors' memories.

Papa's refusal to give up his shoelaces and his arrest are based on a survivor's memory of her own father speaking out before his arrest in the town square. Ruth and her fight to survive stands in for the fight of all these survivors.

Studying these stories and writing about them has reminded me how lucky I am to live in a country that fiercely protects the lives, rights, and religions of all its people. And perhaps kids who read Ruth's story—kids like you—will remember that even young people can fight against big systems, and that history will not forget what they did.

GLOSSARY

Aryan (AIR-ee-uhn)—in Nazi doctrine, a non-Jewish Caucasian person

bubbeleh (boo-beh-LEH)—a Yiddish term of endearment, meaning "little doll"

challah (KHAH-luh)—egg-rich, yeast-leavened bread that is usually braided or twisted before baking and is traditionally eaten by Jews on the Sabbath and holidays

concentration camp (kon-suhn-TREY-shuhn kamp)—a camp where persons (prisoners of war, political prisoners, or refugees) are detained

congregation (kong-gri-GEY-shuhn)—the members of a church or synagogue

consulate (KON-suh-lit)—the residence or office of a consul; a consul is an official appointed by a government to live in a foreign country and look after the interests of citizens of the appointing country

Gentile (JEN-tahyl)—a person who is not Jewish

ministry (MIN-uh-stry)—in certain countries, a section of government activities

pogrom (puh-GRUHM)—an organized killing of helpless people

prejudice (PREJ-uh-dis)—unfriendly feelings directed against an individual, a group, or a race

propaganda (prop-uh-GAN-duh)—an organized spreading of often false ideas, or the ideas spread in such a way

rabbi (RAB-ahy)—a trained leader of a Jewish congregation

shabbat (shah-baht)—the Jewish Sabbath; a day of rest and worship

storm troopers (stawrm TROO-perz)—a member of a group of specially trained and violent soldiers, especially in Nazi Germany during World War II

synagogue (SIN-uh-gog)—a Jewish house of worship

vandalism (VAN-dl-iz-uhm)—intentional destruction or damage to property

visa (vee-zuh)—an official mark or stamp on a passport that allows someone to enter or leave a country, usually for a particular reason

MAKING CONNECTIONS

1. Early in the story, Ruth and her family try to stay calm as the environment they live in becomes more dangerous for Jews. Identify a point in the story at which their attitude shifts. What specific events contributed to this change in attitude?

2. Papa lists two specific reasons he will not try to get his family out of Germany. What are his reasons? Do you think his arguments for staying are reasonable?

3. Ruth risks her safety when she rescues Miriam's prayer book from the fire when the mobs are burning books. Do you think she should have taken this risk? What other course of action could Ruth have taken?

ABOUT THE AUTHOR

Emma Carlson Berne has written more than 90 books for children and young adults. As a descendent of Eastern European Jews, she was honored to write about this chapter in her people's history. Emma lives in Cincinnati with her husband and three little boys.